John Burningham

GRANPA

RED FOX

Other books by John Burningham

Aldo	Humbert	The Shopping Basket
Avocado Baby	Husherbye	Simp
Borka	John Patrick Norman McHennessy	Time to Get Out of the Bath, Shirley
Cloudland	The Magic Bed	Trubloff
Come Away from the Water, Shirley	Mr Gumpy's Motor Car	Whadayamean
Courtney	Mr Gumpy's Outing	Where's Julius?
Harquin	Oi! Get off our Train	Would you Rather. . .

GRANPA
A RED FOX BOOK 978 0 099 43408 5

First published in Great Britain by Jonathan Cape,
an imprint of Random House Children's Books

Jonathan Cape edition published 1984
Red Fox edition published 1990
This Red Fox edition published 2003

11 13 15 17 19 20 18 16 14 12

Copyright © John Burningham 1984

The right of John Burningham to be identified as the author and illustrator of this work has
been asserted in accordance with the Copyright, Designs and Patents Act 1988

Red Fox Books are published by Random House Children's Books,
61-63 Uxbridge Road, London W5 5SA.
Addresses for companies within The Random House Group Limited can
be found at :www.randomhoues.co.uk/offces.htm

THE RANDOM HOUSE GROUP Limited Reg. No. 954009

www.kidsatrandomhouse.co.uk

A CIP catalogue record for this book is available from the British Library.

Printed and bound in China

And how's my little girl?

There would not be room for all the little seeds to grow.

Do worms go to Heaven?

One man went to mow
Went to mow a meadow…

*Little ducks, soup and sheep, sunshine in
the trees…*

I didn't know Teddy was another little girl.

Noah knew that the ark was not far from land when he saw the dove carrying the olive branch.

Could we float away in this house, Granpa?

That was not a nice thing

to say to Granpa.

This is a lovely chocolate ice-cream.

It's not chocolate, it's strawberry.

When we get to the beach can we stay there for ever?

Yes, but we must go back for our tea at four o'clock.

When I've finished this lolly can we get some more? I need the sticks to make things.

When I was a boy we used to roll our wooden hoops down the street after school.

Were you once a baby as well, Granpa?

If I catch a fish we can cook it for supper.

What if you catch a whale, Granpa?

Harry, Florence and I used to come
down that hill like little arrows.
I remember one Christmas…

You nearly slipped then, Granpa.

Granpa can't come out to play today.

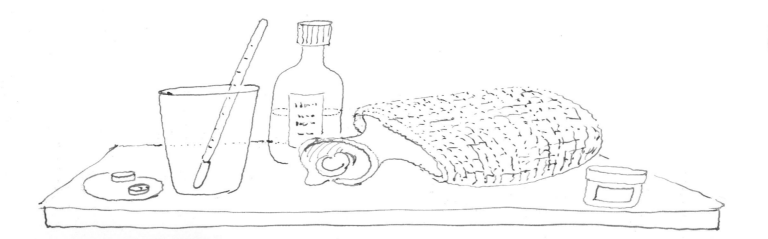

Tomorrow shall we go to Africa, and you can be the captain?